LEVEL 1 READER

Moo Bird

David Milgrim

SCHOLASTIC INC.

For Birdy, my love.

Copyright © 2016 by David Milgrim

All rights reserved. Published by Scholastic Inc.,
Publishers since 1920. SCHOLASTIC, and associated logos are trademarks
and/or registered trademarks of Scholastic Inc.

The publisher does not have any control over and does not assume any
responsibility for author or third-party websites or their content.

This book is a work of fiction. Names, characters, places, and incidents are either the
product of the author's imagination or are used fictitiously, and any resemblance to actual
persons, living or dead, business establishments, events, or locales is entirely coincidental.

ISBN 978-0-545-82502-3

10 9 8 7 6 5 4 3 2 1   16 17 18 19 20

Printed in the U.S.A.   40

First edition, January 2016

Sorry, pal.